Kindred Lamp Posts

Ron Sokol

 FriesenPress

Suite 300 - 990 Fort St
Victoria, BC, V8V 3K2
Canada

www.friesenpress.com

ISBN
978-1-4602-9557-1 (Hardcover)
978-1-4602-9558-8 (Paperback)
978-1-4602-9559-5 (eBook)

1. Fiction

Distributed to the trade by The Ingram Book Company

DEDICATION

We have uniqueness.

When a lamp post first talked to me, I almost ran away.

Almost.

It was a very gradual and cautious process. I did not want to be "that guy." I tried telling my folks, and they were like, "Excuse me? You're conversing with a lamp post? Excuse me?"

Fortunately I had the greatest and most noble side-kick named Jesse. When I visited the lamp posts he would come with me. He was there, he was happy, it was all good, but then he went upstairs to where dogs go, and presumably nearby to where all of us will go, or many of us anyway.

When I get there I am assured Jesse will be easy to find, the beautiful, incomparable golden retriever... And some of my lamp post friends as well, no doubt.

So at this time, and since Jesse is not with me here, nor am I with him there (as yet), some of these stories will now be told.

Preface

"Hello lamp post,

What cha knowing?

I've come to watch your flowers growing.

Ain't cha got no rhymes for me?"

Simon & Garfunkle

Table of Contents

GRETA

My name was given to me because of someone I resemble. I have heard it countless times.

"I vant to be alone…"

Whoever said that was either very pretentious, or was allowed great indulgence, or both.

I do not want to be alone. I accept that many refer to me as "Greta," but it has never been my desire to stand alone. To me, having no companionship is anathema. I like company – be it birds or elements, humans or other creatures, shrubbery or clouds, all are most welcome.

There have been times, such as seemingly endless nights of rain and worse, when I have been greatly tested. I am truly blessed, however, other than for those long nights. In the evening, if I stay well lit, you will notice that I absolutely do not shrink even in my lonely stance, that I keep my bearings even when I can barely make out anything around me.

Sleet, hail, snow, wind, adamant and inconsiderate, full of themselves, without regard to their inconvenience, their demoralizing nature, the pain and real sorrow they aggressively bring.

My favorite time is spring. The flowers come back. Birds are more abundant. In fact, they spend a fair amount of time playing around me, or landing on top of me. I like to think they accompany me. They are part of my being… part of my entourage, dahlings.

Yes, birds have been known to perch on my head. This is my preference by far; to have company and not to sulk.

Greta, to many, from what I gather, was not a lamp post but a woman; a human who lived and portrayed roles in art works. She was known for the expression, "I *vant* to be alone." I understand that she wrapped her face in her hands.

If I could sprout feet, if I could be other than stationery, let me emphasize how greatly I would like to step on to the concourse and greet the many who visit here – who proceed by.

I was meant to be a greeter, not a withdrawer. I don't *vant* to be alone.

You humans have questions. I hear them. Many don't know that an attentive lamp post can read a human mind. We also have superb hearing. Even if you sit at our bases, and think you are having conversation solely with yourself…we may trace your thoughts.

When I hear some of you ask why you are having difficulties, I wish I could tap you on the shoulder. I would like to assure you there is a guiding hand, and that you should not despair.

I've heard questions about why one person is not in love with the other.

I've heard the terrible malady of illness that befalls you, of persons and creatures you have embraced who pass. I have wanted so much on those occasions to be able to make sure you know we are listening, that light and even warmth can be shared with you. To not forsake the clarity of day for the darker alternative.

I do not want to be alone. Nor do I want you to be. Quite the contrary; I would rather be your companion, and you mine.

So, this calling me Greta is a misnomer, but ok, as long as you know I would hold your hand and struggle not to let go, if I had a hand. If I had fingers – the same. I would entwine them with yours. I would be like ivy and you the wall.

We could dance so well together.

Should I have come to know Greta, or should she now come to know me, I would encourage her to change. I would find a way to make her different.

I would change a great deal about her, except her artistry and beauty. Those would remain. I would transform her into a social butterfly, if I could. I would take her hand, wrap its arm around my stem, and have her turn around me. I would say, "Greta, if you will dance with me down the promenade, I will provide the spotlight…"

I dream of what she would say in return: "All right. If you step forward and reach down, with your light to give me a full close-up, then indeed I will do as you request."

I probably would like Greta if I got to know her. But I would change her. You just have to believe that.

The tree nearby, with so many leaves, barks at me: "Shhhhhhh! We are trying to concentrate on the wind. Enough already about Greta! You're missing the whole afternoon!"

VINE

It didn't itch, at least at first. The more it grew, or the more they did, it itched. Never, though. when it rained or when the air was moist.

Fog helps as well.

They decided to have ivy grow on us. All of us.

I guess next we'll be fitted for brick

Well, ok, a bit of an exaggeration when I say bricks. That's simply how we reacted to this… this growth. If you're strapping us with ivy, at least make us a building! Instead, there's a base of dirt, and some of the ivy was already inching up and around us. They stitched it about half way up, and then stopped so it would grow on its own, from there. Upward and around. They put a wire or string, I don't know which, but to right below each of our heads. They also put a collar beneath our bulb in each instance, so if the ivy was aggressive, as some has proven to be, it could not infiltrate our light. This is because our bulb at least is supposed to be inviolate.

Now, you folks shave from what I see. Most of you. We were getting green beards, green body hair, no less! We didn't ask for this, and it grows quite big, and very fast!

To make things worse, the ivy was often childish. Lots of giggles, mischief, and downright asinine behavior. The ivy did not talk to us, other than to say, "Hi, we're here, you are our host or hostess. We appreciate your warm welcome. We will grow up before your very eyes…"

With that we were supposed to stay in our place.

Instead, not one lamp post affected by the sudden advent of this creepy, crawling, uncouth ivy had anything good to say about it. Grumblings were constant… Some, very pronounced.

"If I wanted crawly things all over my body, I'd jump in an ant hole!"

"The ivy makes such distracting noise… Try relaxing, Try communing. We've just become apartment buildings!"

A most unexpected development occurred when some of the ivy began to flower. We had not expected that, and none of us had any prior experience with it, at all.

The color, to our surprise, actually was quite welcome. We saw red and yellow. We also had new visitors – bees and butterflies. On occasion hummingbirds.

"Maybe it's not so bad after all…" was a refrain the lamp posts began to murmur. But, the itching remained most unwelcomed.

With the ivy clinging all the more fiercely and growing incessantly, it caused a level of chafing on our stems (the long part of us – the tall part). Moisture though, as I mentioned, that's key. Moisture… what a relief – ivy itself will then relax (well, relax for ivy, that is).

"Nirvana," is a word we would learn, and a bunch of us said that very word every time we got "a haircut."

Several humans stopped by. They had an interesting device: A bucket, rounded, attached to a ladder, which was part of a vehicle. They came by and shaved back some of the ivy; they clipped it, they cut it.

What surprised us is that the ivy accepted the trimming without any complaint, although a fair amount of it was removed, fell to the sidewalks, was picked up by the humans, and taken away. We have no idea if any of that ivy was replanted. But, the remaining ivy was entirely philosophical about it.

"Seasons come and go. So, too, some of us. To make room for growth we must sacrifice. It is how it is meant to be…"

Sometimes I think that years from now, when the ivy is fully grown, and we've had more time to acclimate, that I will get to know this visitor, the ivy, these leaves of ivy which sprout flowers from time to time… we may in fact become very accustomed to each other. We lamp posts may even think it makes us prettier, or more handsome, more stand-out…

"One big, happy family," chortled Doug, the oldest of the lamp posts. (Our senior spokesperson.)

To be certain, life is fuller now, and busier. There's more going on with all the ivy, and that's a good thing. It takes adjustment and figuring out a way not just to live together, but thrive together.

"We're family… This is good!" said much of the ivy, as they chatted incessantly throughout the day.

I know there is a lesson here: Getting along, getting on. Negativity be damned!

Now we just have to believe it.

And… find a cure for this damn itching!

TATTOO

It didn't hurt really. They put one on one side and one on the other. About eye level, for most of you.

Their dog was missing. I could tell because this little girl had a photo in her hands. I could see it, and she had a leash, but no dog was attached.

She also spoke to me. She said, "Mister Lamp Post, if you see Jason, will you make sure he comes home?" She looked up at me like I could make sure he would go to her house, as if I have any idea where her house is, or can do anything about it.

Someone else came by later that same day. She put a sign up, this one about a garage sale, but she put it facing the street, not toward the sidewalk. So, now I had a poster on my front and on my back for a missing dog, and one on my side about selling a bunch of stuff.

The problem is the wind kicked up. Now, I don't know if wind kicks up or not. I've heard that expression, so I'm using it. Just as well. It was windy, and one of the dog posters came off, and fled down the street. Both of the posters still on me were involuntarily lifting up. They hadn't taped them or stapled them well enough. Actually, I don't know what they should do, I don't know what they did, but the posters were lifting up. Like one of you being pulled from your moorings. And, I sure didn't notice a lot of people looking at either of them.

This is where I don't have an explanation, and never will. You have to understand, the goal each day is to get through it. Some days are less difficult than others, yes, but some are really tough. When there is bad weather, most of you folks stay inside. I am outside, all the time, night and day. I live here. I don't get to go inside, I don't take a bath, I rarely get fed, and no one tucks me in.

Being a lamp post is not for wimps.

Oh, by the way, I am not a he. I am a she, and my name is Betty.

Anyway, I am very glad to report that a few days later the folks who put up the sign for the garage sale, came and got it. Yes, it was still on me, but worse for wear. The last dog poster was barely hanging on. They had not come back, but of interest is that some one did show up.

And…to my astonishment, and I mean that more than you can imagine, they had a dog in their arms. In fact, it looked like the dog in the poster. They peered at the poster, and they looked at the dog, and they talked to each other, and then they used one of those phones you all have, and they made a call and talked to someone. Then they just stood there. They stood there for what seemed quite awhile.

One thing I can't tell is time. Honestly, I don't know if it was a short time or a long time. I just know there's time and that it goes by, it doesn't come back. Also, I can tell you that at one point in time things look one way here, where I am, and at another point things look another way, and you know, there are different things going on around me depending upon what time it is. Different shades of light, different sounds, different activities.

I heard honking. I saw car doors opening very quickly, and a bunch of people coming out of the car, including that same little girl. It looked like a whole family: a mom, dad, brother, another girl, also they had a dog with them.

"Jason! Jason! Jason! How are you doing? We missed you! Jase! Jason!!"

I could tell: These other folks had found their dog, and the family was going on about how happy they were and how grateful, and what could they do for them, and they were high fiving (when they slap hands together, I've seen that before), and I saw a lot of joy, and tears, but I didn't hear anyone thank me for being the place that held the sign.

I don't feel unappreciated exactly, but I had performed a genuine role. Still, no one brought me any ice cream. No one gave me, you know, a slap on the back, or a hug, or anything like that.

So it goes…

Except, well, that's what I was leading to when I started telling you this story.

The little girl comes back awhile later. Next day or two. She comes back and she's got her dog, Jason, and she's with her dad. And he has a sign, a photo. It's a sign of her holding Jason while standing in front of me. And they take that and put it on me. This time they really fasten it so it is not coming off for a long time, if it ever comes off. In fact it is metal, firm and resilient. And, I didn't know this at first, but then someone came by and read the sign aloud: "This lamp post helped find my dog Jason. This is the greatest lamp post ever!"

When the people come by who work on me from time to time...I don't know what you call them, the repair people, that's what I think they are. When they come by and read that note, they look at each other, and I hear what they say. I hear them both say: "We are not taking this down, I don't care what the rule says. This sign stays!"

Like I said, I don't know how to keep track of time, but the sign with that note has been on me a long time now. It is part of me, and I have to say I hope it does not come off, ever. Also, the little girl came by again one time, with her dog Jason. This time she was with her brother, and she looked up and said to him, "I think this lamp post can hear us. I think she can even see us. We should give her a name!"

Her brother snorted: "That's really crazy. Lamp posts can't hear or see!"

"Well, I'm going to call her Betty, after Jason's mom. So Betty, thank you, thank you for helping us find Jason!"

I will share something else (and I know I am going on a bit), but do you ever feel like sometimes the world subsides? Do you know what I mean? The world retracts a bit. How do I say it? The world relaxes, calms down, breathes more easily, isn't all wound up, all crunched up. That's what I'm trying to say.

That's how it felt when she talked to me, and it felt like that for quite awhile. I have to say it is a good feeling.

They put in two new lamp posts nearby, and I got to talking with them. They asked me about this location and what it's like and a bunch of other questions. I said, "What I can tell you is that it isn't easy here. There are some tough times, some harsh weather, there is, but whatever else, I can tell you, if you can help someone or something in some way, if you can assist someone to find something they lost, or give them some shelter or light or warmth, if you can do something for someone else, it really doesn't matter where you are. It's more important what you did."

They didn't understand, I could tell. They were like, "What? How can we help someone, or them or... What are you talking about?"

So I told them the story about the little girl and the dog, and they have asked me to tell them that story again, on occasion. They seem to like hearing it, and I still have the sign on me.

It's my tattoo.

Oh, yes, it does surprise me that her dog's mom's name is Betty, which is my name. If I could shake my bulb in a surprised fashion, believe me, I would.

Just so you know: I am very proud of my tattoo.

SPIRIT

There is nothing unique about grief. Don't wear it like a special shawl, dear. No one is impressed. No badge of honor, that. You are expected to remain, show up, be what you are, hold steady. That is our charge.

I said this to myself time and again, through the night.

Where I am, in this neighborhood, I have wondered why it is important for me to shed light when no one is around. Virtually no one anyway.

My primary company, other than squirrels and occasional birds, my primary company has become porch lights.

But, I am near a house where a gentleman lives with his wife. I have seen them both. They walk at almost the same time each morning. For years, many years, they walked a dog. One day there was no dog. That's when I lost track, except on those occasions when the man would turn on a lamp in the house, or the lamp remained on and I would see him at two in the morning, three in the morning, four. I would see him sitting. He was doing something, looking at something. He was writing I think, or is that typing? Yes, yes, he was typing. And on occasion he looked outside, on occasion he looked at me.

Then one night I must have been dozing off, or certainly not concentrating, and suddenly there was the man, right in front of me.

He spoke: "Lamp post, you have kept me company. Did you know that? In you, seeing you, the constant that you are, that you have been, did you know you have been a companion?"

He sat on the base that surrounds me. He was drinking from a cup.

"Early, even for coffee… You know some drink coffee to wake up, or to stay awake. My friend, I will drink this coffee, go back in, and fall asleep…"

He sat for a while longer, without speaking, just holding the coffee. I had the impression he wanted to say something else, or say something more, but he got up, and abruptly walked back to the house.

The next night I saw him, and he waved. A couple of times. And on this occasion I saw his wife, looking out at me, and then looking at him. She seemed not at all certain what it was she was looking at, or why. In fact she pulled down the blind. A little while later he pulled it up, and winked.

They still walk together, just about the same time every day. I worry if I just see one of them walking, not the other. It is always a relief to see both of them, walking together.

The light does not go on as often in the middle of the night now.

Not sure why.

The man never came back to talk to me again, except once. He had a container of some kind. He sat at my base and clutched it with both hands. He said something to it. He talked to this container. It looked like a gift-wrapped box. Then he walked nearby, down the path a bit, and sprinkled its contents around. He kept talking, saying something. Tears were abundant…and gradually he cast the contents out of the container across the lawn, the bushes, the trees, the other plants, and over the soil.

When he walked by me into his house he had a very, very serious look on his face. He stopped, came back, looked up at me and said, "Keep an eye out for him. His spirit is here."

I felt there was something I should do. I wanted to make sure to do exactly what he wanted me to, but I did not know what it was. Except, well, it is hard to talk about. I am shy about mentioning it, but...well, on occasion, I think I see the dog. It is hard for me to say, but I think I see the dog, or hear him, or both.

Maybe he is right here. Waiting to go on a walk, keeping an eye on the house.

Like I said, the light rarely goes on in that window during the night any more.

The man and the woman walk together. She sometimes does look at me, with what seems to be a question in her mind, but she never talks out loud. He, well, he shrugs. I do notice he puts his arm around her more now when they walk, and often they hold hands.

I wonder if they ever see the dog as well, or is it just me? Some kids might see the dog, or hear him, but kids are different than adults. That much I have learned.

CHILD

His hand was steady, meticulous. Her eyesight superb. "She could thread a needle," I heard him say, "even while doing so many other things."

Part of what makes me who I am, I should say *what* I am, and how I appear, is her. She gave a lot, of time, effort, focus, strength, and I dare say, love.

His importance is equal. Much bigger strokes though. His was to hammer. His was to forge. Little in the way of anything delicate or precise. So if you say, "Well, he's the male…" it explains little to me. He was fierce like she was, but in a different way.

And they clashed.

I was their project, their "baby."

They talked, and they argued. Scribbled. Crossed out. Re-did the drawing. Looked at plans. Yelled. Fought. Bickered. Intermittently loved each other.

One night she remained through sunrise. She had a silver disc that made interesting music sounds. She played the same melody several times. She sang. At times she cried. She drank something. I do not know if it was wine or water. She talked out loud to herself.

He arrived later in the morning with very keen eyes. He studied what had been done. He lightly touched several parts of me. Sat down, put his hands on his knees, and spoke out loud. "Well woman, I compliment you. I must say, I am amazed. Truly. And you, lamp post, you are blessed by her artistry. She is more mother to you, probably more parent to you, than I could ever hope to be!"

Then, just as abruptly, he left.

Unfortunately, I have no mirror. I don't know what I look like. I have never known. When I was being created, clattering is a distinct memory. Sounds of clattering. Sounds of tapping; sounds without sounds; sounds of concentration; sounds of navigation around my base; sounds of careful, meticulous work. Scraping, sanding, patting.

There is one thing I learned – I have two arms. They are like the letter U. She was much more involved in the overall design, as far as I can tell. She did more work on my nuances. His role too was critical. I think my ability to stand, my root and stem, are his product. My fortitude, that comes from him.

One did not dominate. They collaborated. Oddly, though, I feel a greater resonance with her. She spoke to me throughout the process – he made utterances. She used finer tools, more precise devices, and took a noticeably more delicate and warmer approach.

He embraced me with arrogance. He would hit me with his open hand, he would salute me. She would embrace me, she would admire my coming into being.

Incredibly, and I mean it is so, so surprising to me, when I was placed at the street corner, when I was done, when I was unveiled, it was he who had tears in his eyes. It was he who was most outwardly emotional.

I was part of a remodeling project downtown, near the main square. I was to be attractive and tall, intelligently designed, but still very utilitarian, particularly in the evening. I am lit from eight at night, except in summer when it is pushed back to 9:00 p.m., and stay lit till five in the morning. I am to shed ample light, be brilliant, assist those walking, even those driving – by shedding plentiful light, and at the same time I am expected to be statuesque.

All of this I heard many times before I was transported. I therefore took (and still) take myself very seriously.

The speeches were complimentary, but what I remember most is how I am the collaboration of two people, whose names escape me, but who I know as her and as him. I know also that for the most part they are very fond of each other.

"This lamp post is our child. May she be bright and of great benefit for many generations!"

It's when he said those words that I saw the biggest tears in his eyes. I saw them escape from his eyes in dramatic release.

I have tried ever since to think of them standing there, so that I may always make them proud, so that I may always be their child, even as I grow older. They feel similarly, I think it is safe to say, even as they leave me here to fend for myself.

This man and this woman visit regularly. From time to time one or the other arrives alone. They always seem very proud. I just wish I could thank them.

I have come to the conclusion that what I am to do is be good at what I am, and that is how I can best show gratitude. I am to think of myself, in part, as their legacy. And I am to provide real light to others. I am their child, after all.

DISADVANTAGE

There is absolute and real disadvantage to being unable to speak.

I am also unable to bend over, to sit with you, or even audibly utter a sound.

My role, my raison d'être, is to stand, in fact stand tall, to shed light, to provide a place to lean against, a signpost for directions, among other functions. I am not expected to have feelings. And whether I do have them, or I do not, I am not expected to express them. I have no eyes from which to shed tears.

Nor, as far as I can possibly tell, can I leave my place and take time to walk the street, or even clasp my hands to pray.

When Marla began to deteriorate, there was such a feeling of helplessness. We knew she was coming apart, that bolts, connections, the paint; nothing was in synch. We communicated among ourselves, in what is our native tongue. We reached out to her.

Now, please, you must understand, we don't make sound as you may expect it. There is no lamp post any of us knows of who has a mouth, or any lamp post who has visible ears.

But we can communicate. We do, and we hear each other.

Whales have sound.

You don't probably believe me, but flowers have sound as well.

So do, as well, the sidewalks, trees, even windows, yes, yes, windows. I can't entirely explain it to you, but there are ways we are able to hear each other, whether we see each other or not, whether we are adjacent to each other or not. There is, however, a temporal limitation. I cannot communicate for more than a certain distance, and it is particularly difficult to communicate with a lamp I cannot at least observe in the distance.

She had been there before any of the rest of us. She was contagiously positive, outgoing.

About six weeks ago, some forty-two earth days, Marla's lamp flickered a great deal, and was on a very low ebb. She seemed to be drooping. We are not sure if the ground was coming out from beneath her, or she was coming out of the ground, or both. We just sensed that she might literally fall, and that nothing would prevent it.

Her sound became less and less, to the point we could barely hear her, no matter how hard we tried. And, finally, she buckled. A metal plate fell off. She was either scratched or tarnished…or both, in no small part by time, by the seasons, by that which is inevitable.

What is it like for you when you see one of your own starting down the last road?

"Marla, if you can hear me, and I think you can, if you can make sense of what I am saying, we are all asking mercy for you. We are all asking that they come and take care of you."

There was silence.

Then…

"Wait, did you say something Marla?"

"Yes, it's me. I am conserving any energy I have left. I know I need repair. I know it well. I have hoped it will come. Should it not, or should they make another decision, is out of my hands. I have had a very good light! I have brightened more than you can ever imagine."

Marla's voice went silent. I could tell she was very emotional.

There was an enveloping, palpable, long passage of silence.

To you, to those of you reading this, may I please again ask: What is it like when one of your own starts down the road to the end? Do you catch him or her? Do you sit beside? What do you do?

I have seen it among the birds. I have seen it, and of course I have seen it among yourselves. You walk by me, you sit near me, there are some who are mourning. There are some who are quite ill. And there are quite a few, who like Marla, are praying for restoration, although it may not arrive.

It is such a disadvantage not to have a mouth, not to be able to speak out loud. If there is one thing I can say, you are so lucky, you humans, who can speak in actual sounds to each other. You should do so as much as possible, if there is pain in your heart. You should not keep that pain to yourself. God forbid you are like a lamp post, who is to stand straight and tall, who has no actual tongue, nor eyes to make tears, nor arms or hands to hold another.

"Marla, is there anything I might do to be of any assistance? Anything?"

After a few moments, Marla said in a very urgent but hushed tone:

"Shine brightly, every chance you can!"

She was taken away a few days later. I have yet to get to know her replacement. The most telling thing is how so few seem to notice, and how most everything carries on as before.

God, I just wish I could talk to someone about it. I don't want to keep all this to myself.

KISS

Maybe it's because she kissed me. She put her cheek against me, looked up at my bulb, and kissed me.

There is a gentleman nearby who plays the accordion. He has done so for years.

Usually he is here when they're eating, drinking, conversing in the cafes, while sitting outside. He is very happy. He sings. They give money to him, into his open case. He strolls up and down the sidewalk, then turns and repeats it. I wish I knew his name.

He leaves when most of them do, but comes back when it is less light and the crowds come back as well, eating and talking, drinking and comparing notes.

There was a remarkable occasion…I am not sure just what happened, but I thought I saw different colors. I thought I saw bells marching or floating around me. I could swear I swooned, that my very body was bending over, swaying… that I was dipping my head down to one of the tables.

Then when I sprang back, to again be staunchly standing at attention, I reached up and felt as if I grazed the sky. I think so…

Was I caught in some kind of whirlwind?

What is going on?

I saw her, the woman who kissed me. She was dancing…or waltzing. That's it! She was waltzing, alone but among the crowds. I saw her. She was giving out flowers. Many were smiling and watching her. She was barefoot.

The gentleman with the accordion was watching her as well. He played louder than usual. He played with as much emotion as I have ever seen.

She danced toward him, then she danced around him. He turned slowly with her. They did a full circle. He put his head back, and she offered her hands to him. As he moved forward, the crowd made way for them. He played so beautifully, and in turn she was dancing so gracefully.

Rarely had I ever seen all those at the tables paying this much attention, instead of talking among themselves. They all watched. They too were smiling. Some were taking photographs.

Several pointed at me, so I posed as well. I was part of this portrait, this... this moment, these moments.

I felt as if I were holding a violin. I felt like I too was part of the music -- part of making the music. Like me, the fountain nearby was more alive than ever, its water gushing giddily into the air. The park benches became like hands applauding and welcoming passersby. The flowers around the fountain leapt into the air , to nonchalantly then return to their bed as if with umbrellas.

It all started when she kissed me.

I have wondered ever since what it must be like for you, when you kiss, when you love, when you feel great affection for each other. I have wondered how challenging it must be at any given time to stay rooted, to stay in place, to remain where you are. To not dance, to *not* sing.

The gentleman with the accordion was right next to me, his eyes brighter than ever.

He looked up to the heavens, and said something, but I could not quite tell what it was.

She was on tiptoes, her eyes closed, and she was smiling, hugely smiling.

I have never felt so distracted in all my years.

One of the other lamp posts shouted, "Hey, don't topple over, old boy!"

Another quipped, "When you wake up tomorrow with a terrible bulb ache...don't come cryin' to us!"

All I could think of saying was, "Am I dreaming? If so I don't want to wake up!"

"You are not dreaming," she whispered.

I heard her.

"*We* are not dreaming," she shouted.

I heard cheering, I heard clapping, I heard a sound that I could not identify. I believe that you call this "pure joy". Is it rapture? You call this rapture?

It is a sound that I am unable to describe, but that I long to hear again... and again.

It is the sound from the heavens, our endless ceiling, from up there!

Rain, consisting of musical notes and happiness. Plentiful. Seemingly endless!

Rain... torrents of joy. No one should have an umbrella on this occasion. No one should cover him or herself. This is the rain that will bring us forth, that will help us grow!

BLUE

This is most unnerving.

I almost feel accosted.

Yes, I recognize him. He has been a frequent visitor, and has shared with me what ails him. I understand and have seen it, and I get it. I do. So let me introduce myself. I am Edward. I don't think I have a last name. For quite some time now I just have been Edward, and at times "Eddy."

My frequent, well, most frequent visitor is named Sean. He really has fallen for this woman. He just likes her so much, but it is not working out.

He comes and talks out loud and listens to music and writes, and sometimes he calls on the phone, and sometimes he draws and sometimes he sings. There is one song he sings more than any other. He has told me about it so incessantly. It is called "Mister Blue," and it was recorded long ago, in the 1950s he says, by a group called the Fleetwoods. And he plays it for me – I hear it. I have heard it many, many times, and sometimes when he is playing it, and someone walks by, they wind up dancing with him, and they may not know the song, and he always has a hat on, and sometimes he brings a cane so it makes the dancing a bit more alluring, and then he thanks them, after which they walk along and disappear. The other persons always disappear.

He is left, and then he sings the song, time and again:

"Our guardian star lost all his glow, the day that I lost you…He lost all his glitter the day you said, no… And his silver turned to blue. Like him I am doubtful that your love is true, but if you decide to call on me, ask for Mr. Blue…"

On this occasion he arrived shortly after the sun had relinquished the day. He was dressed nicely, all in blue with a flower in his lapel, and a hat, a cane and tears in his eyes, tears rolling down his full face as if paint down a canvas, and he seemed not himself, he seemed a bit influenced by things, or something I don't understand. I am a lamp post, I am not a human being, I don't fathom this broken heart business, I don't.

When he showed up he asked if I would mind if he then climbed all the way to the top of me, on a ladder he brought with him, which he then proceeded to do… and took off the top of my hat, and inserted a large, blue bulb, so that I was showering decidedly blue light… I felt most self-conscious, and also saw his searing pain, I believe you call it sorrow, and he stood in front of me. As people walked by he sang, quite melodically, quite well, he sang more of the lyrics of the song:

"I'm Mr. Blue…wah a wah oooh…When you say you love me (ah, Mr. Blue), Then provin' it by goin' out on the sly. Proving your love isn't true, Call me Mr. Blue…"

Until at that point he fell so hard on the sidewalk.

It was errie. Unnerving. He eventually sat up and said to me (no one else was there), he said to me, "Well Edward, here's another nice mess I've gotten myself into…"

After which he disappeared into the night, and did not come back for several days.

When he did he was quite somber. He was not dressed as before. My light, my white light, had been restored. The blue light had been removed.

Sean spoke, "You know I was not sure you listened or heard me, or that you had any sense of anything. I understand that you are a metal object, that you have no…no…inner self, no consciousness – that you are not able to comfort me in the sense of putting a hand out to me, or holding me, or even saying anything in return, but truth be known you give me great comfort just by being here… a constant. I really have appreciated it. I want you to know that, and I apologize that I have not been as upright as you might prefer, have not been, and am not, all that I could be, or would be, if I was…what I most want to be. Remember…remember please, I am Mr. Blue."

He sat, his hands in his face. He sat for awhile, and I heard his breath. He left with both hands in his pockets, hunched over, as if he were cold.

After that, I never saw him again.

One day a woman came by, with several others. They looked up at me.

"This is the lamp he wrote about? This one?"

"Yes, the photograph – it's this one for sure. This is the one. He said this is the blue lamp, the one he connected with."

"For goodness sakes, stop blaming yourself Ginger. You know well enough he made his own choice, and that's that. There is much…far too much to do and life to live. Do not blame yourself!"

Ginger has red hair. She is "stunning," I guess you would say. She looked up at me with a weariness in her eyes. She said, very kindly, "He wanted me to thank you. He asked that I come here, tell you he really meant what he said, that you were strong and true, and that he will always be Mr. Blue…So thank you, lamp post…Is it Edward? He called you Edward?"

I did not flinch. I did not flicker. I heard what she said. I had a feeling that I had never had before. I felt what it must be like if your light goes out, yet I showed no sign of understanding, or hearing, or of connecting.

"He also asked me to sing that damn song," she continued. *I'm Mr. Blue… wah a wah ooh…I won't tell you…while you paint the town…a bright red to turn it upside down. I'm paintin' it too. But I'm paintin' it blue…"*

"He asked me to sing it to you, Edward, and I wanted to grant his wish… You are listening to me, aren't you?"

CONVERSATIONS

I can't explain why…but two men wearing uniforms placed a device a few feet from my base. They did this last night. No one was in the vicinity, as best as I could tell.

They tested it.

Each spoke, from different locations, from different places. One spoke in a soft, hushed tone.

Then they pressed another device. They had plugs of some kind in their ears. Each was very serious. I detected no mirth whatsoever. They spoke often, at one point huddling together like birds.

It was all quite interesting.

The next day they returned. To that point I had overheard three conversations that were picked up on the device.

One was a young woman who was roller-skating with a young man. She said, "I don't want my parents to know."

He replied, "I'm not going to tell them. How would they find out?"

"You don't know my sister. She'd turn herself in, if she thought she did something even *slightly* wrong!"

"But there is nothing wrong with what we did. We were careful. It's ok Sarah, really…"

"I know, but it would really piss off my parents. You know how they are…"

It sounded like he kissed her on the cheek, and gave her some kind of assurance. Their conversation ended – at least there was nothing more that I could hear.

The second dialogue was very unsettling. It was not long after the first. A woman, in earth years maybe forty-five, fifty, was crying. I remember this because she sat right next to me on the bench, and her friend put her arm around her.

"I don't want to die. I don't want to leave the girls. They don't know if the chemo will work. They can't assure me one way or another."

Her friend also was tearful.

"Come on, let's get to the house. I want to put on a good face for the girls…"

That afternoon, I believe the conversation that the two men were hoping for was recorded. Ah, so that's what this is, a recording device. They rewound it, and played the sound three times. They nodded to each other, speaking very energetically. The device was then put back on me.

This is what the voices said on the recording: "They do an autopsy they'll find the bruises. They'll figure it out…"

"Calm down! First, he drowned. The waves pushed him. He could have been bruised then. They're not going to associate people with any of this. He had drug problems, remember that!"

A silence followed, broken by, "I don't like it. I really want to leave for a while, but I think that will seem suspicious. Oh, hold on here… Look, you see there…that's the kid and the homeless guy with his dog. Let's get out of here!"

The young boy knew the homeless man because he lived nearby. Well, I should say the man did not live here exactly, he exists. The boy learned that the man at one time worked in a church. Sometimes people recognize him and seem very surprised. I heard different people ask, "Father Lou?"

He was, the man is, as they say, disheveled. He laughed for no apparent reason. He shouted, often as if lecturing. He would say loudly, "In the way of the Lord you will find all the righteousness, all of the light, indeed where you belong, where you can say at last you are home, my sweet angels!"

He is a very weathered figure. He would stand near a lamp post, on a raised area. He would hold a book in his left hand, and proclaim, "You may fear me, but not Him. It is He you should pay attention to. Don't mistake the way I look for anything other than an effort to force you to heed what *He* asks me to say…To test you! It is not the messenger to whom you should pay attention – it is *this message!*"

The two men who put the device on me, who wear uniforms, talked to the tattered man about a few days ago. Talked to him, and then placed some kind of metal brace between his hands. When they each grabbed an arm, the dog began barking. The man cried out, with searing pain, "No! No! That is my one solace! That is my final friend!"

The young boy, perhaps ten years of age, kneeled down. The dog came to him. I heard the boy say, "I will have your dog, sir, when you return here. I will have him…"

The man coveted the dog. He and the dog were always together, including when they slept under or near the lifeguard station. Patrols often found them, which meant they had to move. I saw him more than once cuddled up in the ice plant with the dog under his arm.

The boy liked the dog, and the dog liked the boy. This I can sense, I can see from here. Sometimes the boy brought food to the man, as well as food and water for the dog.

The young boy's father is a very tall, imposing person. He reminds me of the tallest lamp post or tree, hovering above others. Thus, whether he wanted to or not, he had to look down at others.

On one occasion he walked to where the man and the young boy were seated. He spoke to his son in a language that I did not recognize. In turn, the boy said to the tattered man, "I am going to my house now with my dad...I will see you again."

The father of the young boy then spoke sternly to this forlorn man. "You should get help. I understand you were at one time Pastor at the church. Can we not help you?"

The man picked up his dog and shuffled away, saying nothing.

Two days passed since the man had been taken away. The boy came out with the dog, looked for him once more, but did not see him. Then suddenly I noticed... the man was there, brought back by the same two men who had removed him.

"We can't hold you. If you have told us what you saw, fine. You understand that a young person is dead – you know that much..."

"I just want my dog. I saw what I told you. Leave me alone. I must get my dog back!"

They left the man sitting nearby. He seemed lost. He seemed to be trembling.

Later that afternoon the young boy came out of his house with the dog on a leash. He saw the man asleep on the bench, who then awoke. His eyes opened wide when he heard the dog barking. He sat up very quickly, his mouth full of unkempt teeth. He laughed. He laughed and shouted "Hallelujah! Thank you Lord!"

The reunion brought tears from the man. The boy stood a distance away, smiling.

"You have to, you have to just let me hug you, one time – Or put my hands on your shoulders and thank you so much, thank you so much, so much, you are, praise the Lord, you are very kind..." the man said to the boy.

Some people were watching. The man turned to them. "Lest ye ever doubt that God is merciful, that He does not care how you look, but who you are, that he takes care of each of us, even one like me..."

Some of the listeners chuckled.

The man continued, "Yes, I saw what happened to the young boy who died. I told them. I told them he was brought here, carried to the sea, taken there and left. They took him into the ocean, they did, two of them, the agents of Lucifer, and they left him far off the shore!"

Soon it was just the man and the dog. The boy went back to his house, and the group who had been listening went their way. But, word was out. Word was out that someone may have had something to do with a possible murder, and I could sense, I could very well tell, the two men who were most concerned…would be back. How that came about, however, was not what I expected.

For lamp posts the still of night is a wonderful time. We can hear ourselves light. You, on the other hand…you call it thinking. Our very being is to shed light, as it gets darker out. We can hear very, very well, and we are wide-awake while many of you sleep.

"Get him! Get him now!"

The two I saw the other day were upon the tattered man. The dog was barking. One of the men kicked the dog. It looked like the tattered man was going to be stabbed. It looked like – --

Wait… wait… There's shouting… Both of the men who had placed the device on me, both of them came from somewhere. They must have been hiding. Quickly they were on the two young men, fighting with them, but they were no match. One of them tried to flee, but was caught. There were others there now, uniformed. And suddenly… lights, a lot of lights, someone has a camera.

"You have the right to remain silent, whatever you say may be used against you…"

As quickly as it happened, all faded back into the night. All faded back into the next day. A curtain down, a curtain up, on the same or similar stage.

Commotions are unusual here. This situation I remember well. It was very sudden. It was very intense.

By morning, however, all was back to what you may consider the more customary routine.

My light dimmed.

Sea gulls began to make their presence known, by sight, by sound, by number.

And soon…bicyclists, people walking…and dogs with their owners and friends.

The young boy, with his father in tow, came out to see the man and his dog. They all were smiling today.

"You helped get the bad guys, right?"

"I hope so. Truth is, they got themselves! For ye shall reap as they shall sow!"

The boy's father stood very tall. "We brought you some coffee, we brought some cooked chicken for your dog, and we'd like to ask you to at least eat this breakfast we made for you…"

The man took a deep breath. He reached up and gestured that he wanted the boy's father to give him a hand.

"I'll have the coffee, yes sir. I will eat the breakfast, yes sir, I will. And you know…You know…The Lord told me if I saw you again, the Lord told me if I saw you again, to tell you I think I could use help. If you have some help for me, I think I could use some help."

The young boy's father grabbed the tattered man's hand, and was still holding it as he spoke. "We will help you, but as you know well, the greatest help you must find is within yourself."

They man nodded as if an acorn to a tree.

Now, I think, I am not sure, I think sometime later I saw the same man again, but he was different. He was dressed in an outfit. He wore a black shirt with a white collar. There were others with him…and the dog, I recognized the dog. They strolled by like others do, in their own world.

At that moment, I really wished I could talk out loud, could readily move about. Instead, I shone a bit more brightly that night than I can ever remember, and without even trying.

In fact, I felt like a beacon.

Some times… I still do.

FLAMBOYANT

Of course some are more flamboyant than others, but none to our collective knowledge (and there are thirty of us in this park), none like Reginald, or "Reggie" as he prefers to be called. Nor have we ever known of a lamp post who has more *utter gall.*

You won't believe me, which is fine, and I would just as soon you did not. Nor will I reveal where this park is located, although Joseph Strauss figures in it, that much I will tell you, because many of us have concluded Reggie is a product of that mindset, that lover of music and women and finer things, himself rather extravagant.

"Mom, is that lamp post tiptoeing over here?"

"My…my word, it does seem to be!"

Reggie found a way to literally release himself from his base and roll, well, it is hard to describe; it was a combination of walking, tiptoeing, and rolling upright. To say he had and has a mind of his own is a luminous understatement.

When the young mother and her daughter approached park security, and fretted about a moving lamp post, the guards not surprisingly gave it no credence whatsoever. But since it would happen on other occasions, five all told, a bit of a legend arose, and a film was done. A group of people would remain in the park at varying hours to catch a glimpse of the freakishly alive lamp post. Tee shirts were sold. Poems written and recited. A web site exists to this very day about the meandering lamp post…

I digressed. Sorry --

It is not just his moving off of the base and returning that I want to share with you. Let me be clear. The typical lamp post consists of certain components. We have specific uses, and strive to fulfill those responsibilities: Location, strength, stature, aesthetic, light, companionship, to some degree shelter, and a place for reflection. Granted you may not agree with each of these uses, or find them in your own experience, or perhaps you have other views of us...

We simply are a bit special, not to be immodest. We are gas lamps.

There is the stem of course (the post, fine, if you must), the ladder rest, cooper internal (to be technical, pig tail and fair nuts as they are called), adjustable air shutter, on top of the orifice (which may be natural gas and which includes a valve placed just beneath the head), the lamp encasing which I call the burner head (and which is associated as well with the burner tip, the burner venture – hope I am not losing you), and then with our hat, a rain shield on top of that, and of course the finial. It is the finial that can be quite a bit of fun, topping each of us in some impressive manner; decorative and inspired, tall and pointed, or a variation that a wonderful imagination can help to enhance.

At one point Reggie managed to have himself painted orange, very light orange on the post. His hat is unlike any of ours; it's multi-colored, including stained glass. The burner tip are bulbous compared to everyone else's, and he has ribbons tied around his neck (best way for me to describe the area from the post to the lamp encasing), and suddenly a finial depicting Cupid shooting an arrow.

None of us know how Reggie got these configurations, nor will he tell us, nor has he ever. When he does speak to us it is in a droll, condescending manner, as if his words come with the light tap (or slap) of a hand-held scarf.

Equally maddening is that he fancies himself unusually romantic. He has tried to be amorous in the manner available to lamp posts with *every* female lamp post through out the park. There is not one who has avoided his attention, overtures, flirting, light batting…well, what for us would be considered bulb (as in eye) rolling behavior.

I have worried that some may be envious of him, and so I try to remind my brethren to take stock of all their blessings, their own uniqueness, not to lose sight of their good fortune to have this place as our home, this lovely park. People walking through often are humming or whistling. There are occasions when bands and orchestras grace us with their melodies, accompanied by sizeable crowds.

"Reggie, I do have one question, and would appreciate your letting me know: Are your mom and dad with us, somewhere still? Are they familiar with how you have grown up?"

"Well… All right… If you must know, father is in Russia with mother in Red Square. I had enough of what it is like there to know the last thing on earth that I want to be is staunch, like them; stuck in the mud, pale, bland, utterly and solely utilitarian. Instead, I blossomed. Show me where it is written that when a flower blooms in the garden, he or she must assume the same posture, color, and semblance of all the others…Show me!"

There was derisive laughter among many of the lamps in the park.

"You misunderstand me, Reg. We would not want you to be other than as you are. We admire your pluck. We have curiosity is all…And we wish you well in your way!"

"I will take that as a compliment. In the interim, you might take note of your own status. You appear to me at any given time to be limpid, not particularly well appointed, and on occasion your light seems rather listless."

"Reggie, why do you utter cruel remarks like that? I salute you, and wish you all the best."

"Well, fine. When we next have some festivities I will not feel at all guilty you won't be invited…"

This attitude of his, the flair with which he holds himself, and the apparent forays to mingle among the humans, however he manages it…These distinguish him. I do not expect you to entirely believe me or to suspend your disbelief. We simply like to think, we lamp posts, that we can and that we do make room for all, that we welcome all whose intentions are good, and whose bulbs shine to help others find their way.

It is a grand credo of lamp posts, in case you are not aware: Shine onto others as you would have them shine onto you.

We have our divas, our charlatans, our grandiose, our very extroverted. Until Reggie I must say I always figured we did not impose upon you, at least not to any appreciable degree.

I caught a glimpse of him peering over the shoulder of a little girl eating an ice cream cone. God forbid if he causes any trouble there!

To each his own you would say.

To each his own lamp, we would reply.

It's just that with some of us, perhaps as with a few who you may know, a lamp shade may make very good sense!

SHELTER

I am convinced they were jealous.

The whispers and remarks under their hoods.

You may not have known just how catty lamp posts can be. Well, guess what…

At times I have thought those who made us infused some of their own personalities into the fabric, the iron, the glass…even the paint. Like your DNA perhaps. Or is it situational? Well, it may be both. You think inanimate objects don't have petty squabbles or issues, or for that matter don't think, don't bother to think, can't think, and even less that we feel? Part of what I am trying to do here is tell you: We feel. Some of us more so than others.

A finch visited on my ledge. There is an area, a shelf, around the beginning of my bulb.

The finch visited, fidgeted, and was nervous. She then abruptly flew off. Came back. Huddled close to the bulb. Picked at herself. Head darting, eyes moving quickly.

This was the female. She is quite small. One day she was accompanied by a male, who was a little bigger. He also was calmer – that's the main thing I noticed. He did not fidget as much. He occasionally inhaled, puffed up, then slowly exhaled. He looked at her. One day they sang. First she started, then he joined.

I liked it. I wanted to communicate with them but it was not possible, though I did manage a few times to actually get my light to blink on and off, when they stayed on my ledge at night.

They had friends. Visitors, I guess you would call them. A few, no more than three at any time. Eventually I realized she was pregnant. In fact, they built a nest, on the right side of my bulb. The wind comes from the left, from north to south. They built the nest on the south side of the bulb, shielded from the wind. They brought a variety of items, some of it wire, pieces of wood, branches, dried leaves or grass. They built a nest, and I was thrilled, I was proud. I gushed.

At night I shone like no one else. This was a bit embarrassing, but the finches – she remained for the most part, not him – they did not seem to care for it. In fact, they squawked. Seems I was making them too visible to predators.

"Look at her," other lamp posts sneered, "all a-flutter, hee hee!"

"Wait until she starts charging them rent!"

"Can you imagine the mess? It will be much worse when the eggs hatch!"

"Well, evidently some are meant to be doormats, even as the rest of us stand tall as lamp posts, hmmm?"

I heard all of the remarks. I heard them, but did not respond. I felt a responsibility to the birds. I also learned about them. There are ways for us, as lamp posts, to be able to pick up information. It's better if I don't share how some of us go about it. You might consider it "hacking." It's innocent, trust me.

Finches are quite small, and have many, many relatives. Did you know they can be smaller than four inches? Their beaks are very strong. stubby, and for good reason.

What surprised me about these two is they seemed to have strayed from the trees. I don't think for a moment they mistook *me* for a tree.

It was always exciting when he left the ledge. First, he would start out flat, a kind of belly-level soaring, flap his wings for a bit to rise up, then turn left toward the ocean. He brought back food when the eggs hatched, some of which I think he found on the beach.

The nest was like a basket. There was a lot of activity around it, between the two of them.

But, a very frightening incident occurred just two days ago, late in the afternoon. She was asleep, and the little ones were very quiet. Out of nowhere a sizeable gull appeared above my bulb, and took a once-around, staring right in at the nest. I have no arms. I have no voice. I have no ability to bend, to shield, to protect. I am a stationery item. And, none of the other lamp posts provided any suggestions, any help, any encouragement at all. In fact, I detected they were watching with fascination at what might become a horrible tragedy.

Some time ago, an older man was lifted from below and onto the walk path here. He was brought up on a bed of some kind. I think what you call a stretcher…There were three people, with others following. They pressed on his chest. They talked among themselves. A siren sounded and others arrived. I noticed quite a lot of people gathering, but not offering any assistance. Not making any suggestions. Not bringing anything helpful to bear. They just watched. Watched and occasionally murmured.

The lamp posts in my vicinity were the same. Passive. Interested in what was really awful, or could be truly awful. To my dismay I share with you, in confidence, that I think some were hoping for a bad outcome, not wishing for safety or recovery or relief.

Is that a trait among you?

Is the way the lamp posts scornfully remarked about my taking in the finches, is that something you do? Petty jealousy? Denigrating remarks and attitudes? Is that something you find among yourselves?

We do not have a God, as you understand it. The sky is our God. The daylight and night-time sky. That is what we observe and worship; most of us anyway. I mean that because I attribute the arrival of the male finch to the sky somehow alerting him. I don't know just what happened, but he arrived shortly after the sea gull made its first pass. He perched right on the ledge. The sea gull scoffed. Her large size compared to the male finch made the odds heavily in her favor. Yet, the male finch hammered his beak into me, pushed his beak forward toward the gull, who winged away and did not come back.

The mother finch woke up, and put her head against his chest. He did not leave for quite some time. I remember that. He stayed longer than he had in a long time. He made no sound. He did not move at all.

She went back to sleep. When the hatchlings awoke, he then took off, but came back soon thereafter with food. He repeated this several times. Then it was her turn.

I looked at the other lamp posts. They knew what I was thinking. They still know.

The finches have completed their time on my ledge. The nest is now gone. When the hatchlings left, the nest, of its own accord, seemed to disintegrate and spray into the wind. Like the finches, it flew out into the world. It went back from where it had come.

It is lonelier without them, but I cherish the time they were here. I liked being a shelter.

I wonder if any of them will ever come to visit, to let me know how things are going. I keep thinking it will happen again.

From time to time, a bird does land on my shelf, and stays for a bit. One night a bird remained until sunrise, but was off. This does not happen with the other lamp posts, at least not much.

Frankly, they don't know what they're missing, and I am not going to waste any time to try and tell them. Being a shelter is good, very much so. I will stand tall on that! Being a shelter to others. Awesome.

COUPLE

"I don't like having bad feelings, but fact is I'm a trash bin. My life is all about garbage. Over time inevitably I reek. There is some level of maintenance, but my life span is not going to be more than four years, five tops. It's a matter of time before I'm discarded, sold for scrap, recycled, whatever!"

She interrupted. "Bin, we have talked about this so many times. Enough, please. You're spoiling a perfectly fine morning…"

"Hmmph! Try being me. There is no morning, noon, or night. Garbage in. Garbage out. Sometimes it don't even all get out!"

"Bin, I know…I know."

"What do you know?"

This is how their ironic relationship has been for as long as anyone can remember.

The rose bush says, "Hey, it keeps 'em young. He complains. She comforts."

The lawn says, "God forbid they sleep at different times… we'd have even less quiet!"

But one day, one day out of the many, one day was *a lot* different.

Three desk lamps came to visit her.

(Oh, sorry, her name is Lyn, and as you have read, his name is Bin.)

Three desk lamps, each about a tenth her size, well not even, maybe a twentieth, gathered around on the lawn. It reminded me of a family of ducks I'd seen. The mom and her ducklings, marching by, in a line, in a row, the little ones following mama…

Bin has a soft spot. That would be the kids. That would be the young ones.

"They haven't got all scuffed up yet. They still have that gentility, that innocence."

He actually got a little wistful, and Lyn, in turn, beamed ever more brightly. Stood taller than ever. Stood out proudly more than even before.

As to poor Bin…well, a lot of us grimace, to be honest. The way they pick Bin up and dump out the garbage, it's not a pretty sight.

"Kills my back every time. But, you know, the best time is the days I'm empty. No trash. None. That's like your weekends. You work a lot Monday through Friday, then you get Saturday and Sunday off. Same kind of thing for me."

But Lyn was giggling about the desk lamps. "Sillies, aren't you all just tiny darlings?"

One of the desk lamps kept going on and off. This was his way of getting Lyn's attention. They call her, by the way, "Auntie Lyn…"

Bin started back with the grousing: "My luck, someday little trash receptacles will come to see me, and they'll say, 'We came to visit you, Grandpa!' As if I have anything to offer…"

"Uncle Bin, you're silly," the desk lamps shouted. This was followed by a lot of mischievous laughter.

It was in fact a great moment for all of us there.

Bin talked about those "kids" for days after that. When Lyn's light was on you heard it; you heard a humming, a happy sound that you hardly ever heard from her, or any other lamp post for that matter.

"You think we'll retire before they come to get us?" Bin asked.

"I hope so," Lyn offered. "But we needn't worry about that now when we're still young. Worry about it later. Or, even better, stop worrying all together. We have each other."

"Those little lamps are going to come back, right? Come back and visit?"

"Bin, if there is one thing I can say…no, two things: They are coming back, and they will never find their way into you!"

All was quiet for a bit, when Bin said, "You know, the fewer ever get into me, like that, like those young ones, the better!"

FREEWAY

It was not until I could see that I realized where I was. Just outside downtown, adjacent to a freeway. One of the few plants nearby is an erstwhile palm tree.

There are cars. At times, many, many, many, many cars. Trucks. Buses. Vans. Vehicles. Motor cycles. Lots and lots and lots of traffic.

You know automobiles make noise. It is not just the person driving who can press a horn. It is the engine. The brakes. The tires. Sometimes they run over an object, and that too makes sound. I've yet to be hit by any objects that were cast into flight, but a few have landed nearby. In fact, one came to rest right next to me. A set of keys. Something is attached, but I can't quite make it out. Also, I recognize keys when I see them because a man in a uniform comes to me, on occasion, and uses two keys. He opens a small slot below, and locks it after he's done. He turns something there. Another key opens a part a little higher up, on my back, and he pours fluid in there. I feel better after he is done and wish I could thank him. I don't like being dependent on anyone or anything, so I tend to keep my feelings to myself. He never seems to have much expression on his face, although a few times I heard him say, "Ok, big boy, drink up!" One time he had a shirt on with a sign that read, "She's with stupid…"

The keys that landed next to me are bent. One of the keys is complaining that she hurts, and that she opens a big house, but now she's lost. "I have no purpose! What if they don't find me? I'm useless! Is this where I will wind up?"

I tried to calm her. "You know, I am stuck here, not where I want to be either. I try to make the most of it. Day or night."

"You serve a purpose, lamp post. What am I – but a key without a door!"

"Have faith you will be found. I am sure given what you did, what you unlock, that they are looking for you."

"Have faith you say? How can I? Look where I am! I fell out of the car, from the window. I don't even remember how… we were thrown with such force. We're all hurting!"

"Key, I have been here a long time. I don't like this location. I get dirty every day. Every single day. I have insects that attack my head when I'm lighted. There is very little to look at day to day. But, I persevere. I think in time I will be moved. I find things to focus on. Clouds. Clouds are a major interest of mine. So hear me out…I believe that this is where I am starting, not where I am finishing up. That's my faith."

"Clouds?"

"You can see them. Look up – up – yes, at the ceiling, the sky."

"The white stuff? I see bunches of white stuff. *So what*?"

"They pass over. They have a much shorter life than you or I, but you know I've never heard any of them complain. In fact, they are often chuckling. They like who and what they are. They come out of water, form into bunches, meander, pass over, and return to the ground. They come back, but not as the same cloud, not in the same form. They become part of all of this – they come back…"

"Your point, lamp post. Do you have a point?"

"Have faith. "

Key did not utter a word that night. In the morning, a stray dog came by, sniffed all the keys, lifted its leg, and was off.

I could hear her crying. I felt so bad for her. I did not know what to say. Worse yet I knew I would start dimming that night. When a lamp post is sad or depressed, and I am now both, it is hard to shed much light. Yes, we have emotions too, and sometimes they show.

The morning arrived with the cars, the noise, the incessant sun…and the more ordinary events that have become what I have to cope with again and again.

And again.

On a few days, there has been a respite. On one occasion, a beautiful parade. Going by were these large depictions, done in flowers. For three full days there were virtually no cars. Instead, a lot of people on the sidewalks, sitting, chatting, eating, waving, smiling, talking.

Once, the whole freeway was shut down. A bunch of people were doing restoration work, including on me, and they trimmed and fed the palm tree. We all were happy. We all felt very refreshed.

There was a third occasion that I remember. Light was coming out of the sky. There was light, then sound, a cracking, sometimes a boom. Cars pulled over. Otherwise, it was very hush. There were torrents of water, and more of the loud booming. Then, these incredible flashes of electrical light. I still do not know where it came from, who sent it, or how it came to be.

"That's lightning, lamp post," shouted the palm tree. "Pray it doesn't hit either of us!"

I remember those occasions well. In fact, they convinced me not to despair. To stand tall, proud, to believe a day would come when I would be moved to a much better location. Like I said, I believe this is just where I am starting, and in time I will be in a much better place.

I didn't tell you about my friend, who was older, who was here well before me, down the road a bit, and one day they took him. They lifted him up from his base, placed him lying down in the back of a long truck, and drove off. He was thrilled. He said, "Finally, I am moving! My friends, I hope to see you again. I know they are taking me to a neighborhood…I hear them talking about it!"

This was not a big surprise to me, but an affirmation of how I feel, what I believe the future holds. I too will be moved to a better place.

Then suddenly, like that, a young boy ran toward me.

"Dad, look!" The boy bent down and picked up the keys. "He's here! *He's here!*"

"Wow…Wait, hold on. Hold on. Clean those off. Look at 'em… Your buddy's filthy!"

The boy was looking at a figure in a baseball outfit, attached to the key ring.

"His body is flat…He's all bended, dad…"

"He'll be ok. We have to get him home and make him well. We found him – that's the important part. We don't have to change our locks, we have our door key, we have to get her cleaned up as well…"

The lamp post had no idea (until then) about the figurine attached to the key. He had heard the door key, the one whom he'd talked with, but no one else.

The key shouted: "They found us! We're saved! I'm going home! Lamp post, we won't forget you. Have faith you said. You were right! Lamp post we won't forget you!"

And soon, just like that…as at birth and at death, life goes on. The cars were thick and ever noisy The palm tree was thirsty for a big drink of water.

I was encouraged, though.

If you can hear me, I will say to you, "My day will come. We all must have faith. I am just like the door key. I will be found. I will get to the home where I belong. Faith is sustaining me, just as it should… In the interim, in this purgatory, there is no lamp post in the whole world that shines any brighter than me. Some who live downtown, who reside under the tall buildings and stars, sometimes see me at a distance and wonder if that is the star who guides all travelers, not a lamp post at all. Or maybe that bright light is a star that indicates God is talking to us, telling us a child is here who can teach us all."

ORPHAN

I am not an orphan!

I'm not an island!

So, why am I stuck here? In an obscure corner, near a wall, a dark, moss-covered wall behind me. I can barely see a thing ahead. It is always this dark. It has been this way for so very long now. What hope is there? It is always extremely cold.

I have shouted into the abyss: "I am a lamp post. I have light! Who brought me here? When is he or she coming back? Tell me, is this Hell?"

"Stop… dear, stop… Please. I brought you here…"

The voice startled me. It is so dark, and there has been so little sound, ever. I began to firmly believe that I was, that I am completely alone. Perhaps like the earth itself…

The voice came again: "Child, I brought you here…"

"Mother?"

"Good, you can hear me. I have been too ashamed to show myself, but please look up…"

The shock of that warmth, the golden light, so perfect, so enveloping. I felt as if I may be released from the darkness. I thought perhaps, perhaps I am going home.

"I am so sorry, my child. I should have come much sooner, and wanted to, with every breath…Just please know that I will never forsake you, ever!"

Stammering, I managed to say, "Thank you, Mother. Thank you… Will you stay?"

"I can't stay here, child. I do not belong here. But, you must know that I am here, that I am with you whether you can see me or not. You must know this… You are not and never have been an orphan!"

My thoughts were scattered. I tried to think of what to say, what to ask…

"What about my father?"

"I did not know him well, and I have lost track. He was tall, sturdy, strong. He was a true light. I am sorry, please understand, I am so sorry that I cannot bring him here as well, but I will keep looking, and I will return, whether with or without him."

Again, my mind was racing. Am I dreaming?

"Mother, what is it like out there?"

"Some of it is wonderful, some of it is warm and comfortable. Some of it is far more treacherous than even where you find yourself today. Some of it is ghastly, frightening, not light at all, but abject and painful darkness."

"After all this time, did you put me here?"

"They did. There are others around you. You just cannot see them because for quite some time they have pushed away any light. If only you knew how many neighbors you have, how many there are around you."

The lamp post struggled for words…

"So, I have something to look forward to? I do have something to look forward to?"

"Yes. And I am coming back, soon! I am bringing your sister with me. You did not know that you have a sister."

As she spoke I began to feel very different. I began to think where I was perhaps wasn't so bad. I began to realize that I may actually have good fortune, at least better than I thought. Suddenly I began to illuminate a much greater area than before.

Her words, "You are not an orphan," meant more to me than you can imagine.

"Mother, come back soon! God speed!"

I do not know how many there are around me. I do not know how many of them also long for their mothers, their fathers, sisters, their brothers. Some of them began to stir for the first time.

Like the earth waking from winter. Like the deer venturing much farther than before. I began to think the universe was worth getting to know, to come out of the darkness, to come forward.

You may think of it as a fish venturing from the water. Like that. I must begin somewhere.

Why not here?

"I am not an orphan!" I yelled with delight. "I am not alone in the universe! You hear me, don't you? You hear me!"

PROFESSOR

"Oh boy, brace yourself…When Professor gets talking, we may be in a for a full day and night of it."

He is the very oldest of the lamps along the boulevard. We call him Professor. He's been known as Professor so long ago that I do not know his actual name.

And so he went on: "Now, lamps in the Greek and Roman civilization, you see, were for security…oil lamps in the main, which were actually fairly long-lasting. The Romans had a word, "laternarius," which meant a slave responsible for lifting oil lamps in front of their villas."

"Professor, did you notice someone painted on you?"

"Excuse me?"

"Some kids I think, younger people. You have two large swaths of green paint, and it looks like a name, but I can't make it out…"

"Goodness. Well, as I was saying…Candles came before incandescent lamps. Remember, we had lamplights in the day, until someone figured out how to ignite the gale remotely. Public illumination, as it were, is associated with the early fifteenth century…"

His lecture continued, but my attention was abruptly cut off by unnerving screams.

"*Oh my God! My God! Help!*"

Three lamps away…one of us suddenly was under attack.

"What is that?! Oh no…noooo!! A vehicle struck her. Oh no…She's bent over. Explosion? Is that an explosion? What is going on?! Someone do something!"

People came quickly, a siren, one of the persons in the vehicle managed to free himself, but was staggering. There was crying, shouting, *oh no no no….What will they do with her?!*

She's a victim!

Actually, we all are. Victims of time, seasons, even of what you call progress. Of vandals, accident, and nature.

Maybe it is harder for trees, because they are subject to insidious predators, some times small even imperceptible creatures. For us, if there is an equivalent I would say it is time, but today we are cared for, and with some regularity; tinkered with, checked, even coddled, and let me be clear, we appreciate it!

Still, the Professor continued on..."Piped coal gas was employed in the first widespread system of street lighting. Now, let me be emphasize," he blathered, "we are not signals. We do not influence the flow of traffic among these humans, by walk or by mobile vehicle of any kind. We light the way and most of us today, most, become illuminated through sensors that tell us it is dark. Of considerable interest is our design. You do know that fatola Fernandina is traditional, and remains quite popular in Spain. It dates, for your information, from the eighteenth century. A footnote please...the name comes from the birth of King Ferdinand's daughter."

"Professor, all well and good, what about our friend? What is happening with her? Is she going to collapse? What are they doing with her?!"

"Ahem...ahem..." the Professor obnoxiously cleared his throat. "My friend, in turn, you know and I know there is inevitability in our existence. Do you know of any lamp post ever that has never failed, or that stands forever?"

Several lamp posts simultaneously shouted, "Quiet! Enough! We can get the history lesson later. For now we have to figure out some way to help her!"

"Suit yourself, but you remind me that to the extent we are family, there is great dysfunction among us," the Professor muttered.

No one at that point gave any further thought to him, let alone later when he continued going on and on. Our thoughts were with Linda. She was the one who was violently struck by the large metal vehicle.

Linda means pretty, in Spanish, and rightfully so. She is a lovely lamp post, just three years of age.

There is something I want to share with all of you: We are helpless, in many respects. We have thought out how we may fight back against vandalism, against it all. If we could create an electrical current, or for that matter if you can for us. We appreciate that some of us have cameras nearby to see what has occurred at any given time. We have compartments that you can open to check on us, to keep us functioning, and you clean us, you dote on us at times, for which we are very grateful.

We rarely can do it ourselves. You think of us as inanimate, and we will not disabuse you of that impression. God forbid you would know that we do think, that we converse among ourselves, that we see in our own way, let alone that we feel. Forgive me, I mean no offense, but sometimes I think of the animals you slaughter to feed yourselves, and I think they know, they feel. They may rise up some day, no?

I will share with you that I was vandalized. I was not lured to a place, or deceived. I did not answer an ad, nor was I kidnapped or taken anywhere. In a fit of brutality, three people hacked me, with instruments of some kind. I knew there was a commotion. There had been a large gathering of humans. There was brisk talking over a microphone, lots of applauding, and a consensus among them of camaraderie, of purpose.

They just flailed at me. I think one had a hammer, a very large hammer. He swung with all his might. I cannot express to you the horrid, unforgettable pain, the shock. And there was another who hit me with a pipe. Finally, the third just was hell-bent on pushing me over, to leave me crashing into the sidewalk, broken for good.

I was not the only lamp post attacked.

Yet, something happened that I will never forget, nor will any of us. We remember it more so than that day or date. A woman brought the marauders, the pillagers, brought them to a sudden halt. She said, loudly and with intense conviction, "My brothers, my sisters, *cease!* Cease your harm! Cease! Show our opponents we are able to seize victory, to make our goals, without destructiveness! Cease! Cease now! Let me float like a dove on your sword. See me there! We will be victorious by number, by substance, by unity!"

At that a great shouting occurred, and the men who were so savagely hurting me, trying to take me down, damaging me with real fervor…stopped. One had second thoughts, but his colleague held his arm.

I do not know what came of them, or what changes they brought, if any. I know that the next day there were what we refer to as doctors treating several of us, hammering out my indentations, removing scars from our surfaces, straightening us out, restoring us to our fine, delicate function, so that we might not just stand tall and proud, but shed ample light.

"Good as new!" said the man, and slapped his hand against my stem.

I still shudder at what happened to me. I share it with you to increase your awareness of our fallibility. We are in need of protection, at least at times. We ask for no sympathy, but remember that we do not ever seek to harm any of you, and would ask that you never seek to harm any of us. Am I not like terra firma itself, which you call home? Would you not want to protect your home, if at all possible?

By this point, the Professor was onto Paris. "In 1878, you recall, the first electric street lights were installed in the incomparable city of Paris, France, and in that same year in London, a city shrouded at times by fog and so obviously in need of our assistance, the electrical arc lamp was placed at various locations…"

The lamp post impacted by a car was blinking on and off. "I'm ok. I think I'm ok. I think I'll make it!"

We breathed a collective sign of relief. We simply were reminded of our vulnerability. Perhaps you understand this well!

STARBRIGHT

The cackling is unbearable. Obnoxious. Stars have quite an attitude! It is, has been, and remains a point of major consternation among lamp posts, virtually everywhere.

First, they constantly remind us, "We stars are always lit."

We are, they insist, at most, utterly modest imitations. And, although most cannot see the stars during typical daylight here on Earth, they remind us they are always shining, that the stars are not simply twinkling. They scorn us because we "take a rest" during daylight.

"Oh you poor, poor creatures. You must shed light during the night… You must get so so tired, poor poor dears…"

So it is we are considered knock-offs, and poor imitations at that. We are not spectacular, they say. We are not magnificent, they snarl. We are like teeny tiny ants compared to them, miniscule specks. We are not even dwarf stars, but mere molecules of metal and wire.

If the humans took real stock of us, then, the stars insist, lamp posts would be obsolete…Inconsequential!

"Have you ever heard anyone wish upon a lamp post? Ha!"

We try not to listen to them. We've learned that upon death, stars are utterly destructive.

They collapse onto themselves, and, in their fervor, their self absorption, their utterly narcissistic obsession, they take space and time with them, if they can. Imagine, dying only to create hell for every one in the neighborhood!

Thus, to the extent stars try to portray themselves as lanterns illuminating the sky, and lamp posts as pinpricks of muffled dots…we rail back.

A friend of mine had a dream in which he escaped from his mooring and managed to travel far away. In the dream he grew by absorbing light from any available star. He came to equal if not exceed them in size, to have a vastness and unmistakable, ominous presence. So monumental was he that he rivaled the very sun itself!

"And why not? My bulb is magnificent," he shouted throughout the universe. "My bulb is a star!"

Of interest is that the sun never denigrates lamp posts. She simply is not as petty as the other stars. She is confident in her place and position. She knows what she gives, what she provides. She shines without requiring adulation. She is, after all, the sun.

Catcalls, that's the expression you utilize. That's what we hear often enough from stars. Insults. Taunts. Little do they know we are a part of a place, a very real place here on Earth. We are not burning lily pads in an endless, unfathomable sky. We take great pride in having roots.

The stationery lamp post would never trade places with a star – ever. We know that's what they would prefer, but wishing does not make it so.

Keep in mind with the advent of lamp posts have come fewer of those looking out to the stars, and seeking guidance there. People here know we will give them guidance, as they traverse the path.

We know well that stars have their place, their history, their resonance with humans. But we are here and they are far, far, far away. Our light does not travel through space and time to make itself known. We require no binoculars or telescopes. Nor space exploration.

We are right here. Waiting to assist you.

Be it known: We want to be your stars.

RESTORE

Part One

"Well, you don't know what you have till you lose it." You folks say that more so than me and or any of us here.

A village that prides itself on charm, history, and culture, that caters to the observant, that a poet would love to stroll through. Each street its own bouquet.

Then explain the dying Victorian-cast lamp post just a few yards away. He was made in a foundry over one hundred years ago; locally no less. He could be restored. After all, you wither too! You may need a replacement part. At least half of you doll-up, color your faces, wear clothes to enhance your presence.

This is not like horses. Retiring them to the pasture, which may be a better life at that point. They deserve rest, calm, the good food. Our purpose is to light, to stand handsome, to reflect years and gradual seasoning. We should not be taken down!

It is painful to see. Gas lamps that were modified and which are now electrical. There was quite a lot of apprehension that we will be recycled, taken apart callously, or used in other creations, long before our time.

Our remaining paint can be removed. It is a process, yes. We will have to be heated, yes, yes a blow torch, followed by a wire brush and sandpaper from top to bottom. Coats of primer followed by finish, yes. It is work. There is cost. It is effort. But, there is good reason for it.

Excuse me then: Sirs and ladies, let's be clear: You have bypass operations! You replace organs with other organs! You reconstruct your own bodies! But, you wouldn't think of doing the same with us, who have stood against it all for over one hundred years? Now that we start to show wear, the so-called ravages of time… we are done?

There is a young man in your very midst who plays professional golf, yet with someone else's heart! He was not cast aside. He is with you, he is contributing.

The conduit and cable can be fitted. Keep us here! It is not a matter of bringing us back to life. It is a matter of showing respect by simply giving us that to which we are entitled: Restoration. Healing!

Isn't your Lord a healer?

For us, it is our primary goal to light the path, far less to look attractive, but we know you often cherish our beauty. I have heard so for years.

The sighs and whimpers, the creaking of our shells, peeling, faltering. Our connections fray. To see it, to hear it, to feel it, to know it is happening, in our very midst, and we have so little that we ourselves can do about it. We rely on you, and in turn we understand you rely on us. What about a two-way street? Please do not forsake us!"

Part Two

The town council met in open session. Our condition, and the decision about us, was taken up promptly at seven. We have an advocate, whose name is Gerald; well-dressed, passionate, with a trim moustache, who spoke eloquently of our history, the consistency of our pattern, the beauty of our creation.

As he spoke I realized his argument for restoration was not meant solely for us.

"Elegance is not replaceable!" His voice boomed. He had photos that were shown on a screen. He had photos of the days when we were being made. Photos of our unveilings. Photos of events in which we participated amidst the landscape, and of course photos at night showing our undeniable, additional purpose.

"You, Wayne, you, Carol…You, each of you, with elderly parents. Would that you could restore them, no? Is this really so different? Would you cast them aside because we have replicas today? Lookalikes that are fitter, you say? Lookalikes that may not require the same level of attention?"

Wayne responded, "Both Carol and I appreciate your determination. The council will decide this, but what our parents have to do with this is too much, really…"

And then, as if the lamp Gods themselves had arranged it, the parents he referred to, who were seated in the gallery, came forward. Wayne was stunned, astonished as his mother and father stood at the podium.

"I will speak for us, son…We have the blessing of many friends here. It is not that much of a stretch to speak of us, and at the same time, these Victorian lamp posts. Times change, we know. Time takes its toll, we know all too well. But, here in this village where so many of us have been born and have lived, and will find our resting places, we have always taken great pride in our surroundings. We have worked so hard in gardens, shops, on the streets, at corners, with trees, benches, with windows, chimneys, and parks. Don't take away from the main avenue that which so defines it. We have heard these lamp posts may be placed among the neighborhoods. Separated from each other no doubt, scattered to Dalehurst, Le Conte, Chatham Way. Uprooted is more apt, from Village Circle, from the heart of this town, perhaps touched-up and planted elsewhere. We ask earnestly that you reconsider, that the newer versions take their places in the neighborhoods, that our longstanding lamp posts, who are quite like friends to so many of us, who we know, for whom we have nicknames, where we have for all of our lives found solace and light, leaned against, met at their bases, and serenaded each other... Restore them. Show them their due, and keep them in place!"

You could hear the light of a lamp post, it was so quiet. You could (in time) hear shuffling, a kind of unease among the council. It seemed as if it was actually time herself speaking to them. It was the voice of an historical heart. It was not the voice of today. It was not youthful, and yet it was utterly child-like. Its innocence was profound, and palpable.

Later, when each of us spent time being restored, each of us, every single one of us, had so many stories to tell. Still, no one came to the hospital room bearing cards or flowers, balloons or well wishes. No one sent any of us a "Get Well" note... but we knew that was the intent. We *know* this is the spirit of our redemption.

When all of us were completed, the village had a celebration. I would not know a "ticker tape parade," I just heard that expression several times. We were so thrilled to be restored. We were so happy to continue to live, to remain, to have our home, to stay here in place.

One of the lamp posts told me, "Until this, I thought heaven was some-where you went after you expired, after you were taken apart. I didn't realize, it is remaining in place with a new coat of paint, with a new set of wires, with a fresh cleaning and restoration."

There are some who preach nearby, at the park. A few who stand on the sidewalk do likewise. They talk frequently about religious matters. For me, and for the lamp posts here in the village, restoration and religion are one and the same.

We have a Cathedral by the way, very beautiful, several hundred years of age, and a group of painters and sculptors who work on the drawings inside and out, who work on the fountains, who seem tireless in their dedication to keep the beauty well maintained.

I would not know, but I believe restoration is among God's favor-ite endeavors.

I also think at some point, being awake through each night, that I should be able to converse in some manner with God. His image for us is much dif-ferent than the image you have, but bottom line, there is one very common belief we both embrace: We should be forever young.

SUSPECT

From looking at them you probably wouldn't expect it. Or well, maybe you would. Look at them long enough. They're definitely different. They've definitely got something going on there.

"Hello Ted, my name is Steph. This is my colleague Frank. We're from the *Evening Outpost…*"

"Fine, all right then. If we're going to do this right, just follow along, observe, take notes if you wish, or keep it all in your head. We can talk about it later, and you decide what to do about it, if anything."

We were at North Harbor and Pier.

The dock.

Boats, some very big, and vessels. Cargo in. Cargo out. It's a city onto itself. A lot of people work there, a lot of people spend a good part of their lives there, and the lamp posts have been present for years.

They found one in the harbor, in the water, half submerged, and figured something happened. This was the second in less than two weeks. This one had tipped over. They weren't sure why. When it happened a second time, you wanted to cover your ears. Everybody, *every*body…has a theory. The rumor that got the most traction is that a group of the lamp posts were ousting others.

"I dunno if you would call it a gang war, or a battle over turf. I dunno. This is the group there, where I'm pointing, there are five of them. They all look pretty much alike. They've all been here longer than anyone can remember, they all work ok, but they're shorter and wider than the two that met with some kind of end-thing, some kind of end- game, I guess you'd call it."

"Can we talk with them?"

"Talk with them? Say what? Well, you can inspect them."

A sea gull nearby said very plainly, "Yeah, yeah, they'll talk with you. They ain't shy!"

Steph could hear this – only she could; the others not at all. She acted nonchalant, as if there was nothing unusual about it.

She went to the group of five, walked in and around each of them. She spoke in her mind. (None of the people she was with had any idea what she was doing. They did not know, nor would they ever know, that there are some who can converse with lamp posts, let alone sea gulls… indeed, it is rather rare.)

"You have an explanation for why those two other lamp posts wound up in the sea?"

The one in the middle quickly replied, "Nope, you?"

"I was just asking. You live here. I'm visiting, trying to figure out how this could have happened, trying to make sure it doesn't happen again."

"Since we had nothing to do with it in the first place, we don't know if it's going to happen again. They toppled over as far as we know. You think we pushed them? You see hands? You think we move around here, is that what you're thinking?"

"Hey, I just asked what you know, that's all, and it doesn't sound like much. If you do know a lot more, seems like you're not going to share it with me. Am I right?"

There was no response.

Instead, the lamp post who had been conversing, one of the five, began to snicker.

"Sun, cold, wet, heat, time, rain, wind, all the elements you know, time being the main, just plain time, and she's asking if those two had help coming to an end. You get that? That's rich!"

"So, it was natural causes? Can you explain why each of them had gashes, both at their bases and part way up their stems? Looks to me like someone was slashing them, that's all I'm saying."

"Lady, you got a lot of video cameras here. Check out the tapes. Now, if you don't mind, it's daytime. This is the part of the day we like to rest, you know, recuperate. The nights aren't real easy, particularly if the air is cold, and full of fog. Come down late tonight, check it out for yourself, but wear shoes that aren't slippery. You fall into the water that's all we need. We'll get blamed because you were wearin' high heels!"

She did in fact return that night, with a cameraman. They had to arrange access to that particular part of the harbor, which typically is sealed off for security purposes by eight p.m. She noticed it was both wet and dark. The atmosphere very unsettling. The five lamp posts were imposing, but all were where she had seen them earlier that day. She knew the videotapes that law enforcement looked at were inconclusive. It was hard to see much of any-thing on them.

"Well, well, if it ain't Sherlock Holmes's mother!"

The lamp post who had spoken with her earlier was talking. "You want maybe we hop around a bit, push a couple trash cans into the water, just for fun?"

She did not respond. What she saw surprised her. "Frank, was that crane there earlier today?"

"You know, I don't think so. That's awful big. I think we would have noticed."

They spent about twenty minutes, and were glad to get out of there. They made a point of finding out whose crane it was, and how it got there.

What they learned was surprising.

"Bob Valentine has a metal plant, makes lamp posts. He does all right. He's the go-to-guy around there, not just to fix lamp posts by any means, but to make 'em."

Turns out the crane is part of Valentine's equipment, and was there for some lifting of containers onto one of the boats, but no one knew why it was there that night, or even how it got there.

With that she went the very next morning to visit Mr. Valentine.

"What can I do for you?"

"We're trying to find out what happened with those two lamp posts. There's some concern they were disposed of… by others perhaps. Just why, we don't know. Our question is with regard to the crane we saw last night toward the end of the dock. What's that all about?"

Valentine turned on them: "You can speak to my lawyer. If I'm under some suspicion, you know, I am not going to take any chances. You people stick your noses all around, and I don't need it. See the door?"

With that he got up, and made sure to maneuver her and the cameraman out of his office.

"He has motivation, and he sure seems defensive, that much I'll say."

But the police and the harbor patrol had already ruled out Mr. Valentine. In fact, they knew what had happened, but they didn't want the details to get out – they did not want the public to know.

The two lamp posts got cancer, or well, what's cancer for them. It's rust, really aggressive rust. It spreads fast, like swarming bees...piranhas, a better way to think of it. Aggressive. Agonizing. Deadly.

The City and the Port don't want that getting out because the cost to replace is very substantial. They are fearful they'll be blamed for not keeping things well maintained even though they are so well funded. To that end, they let all sorts of rumors and stories swirl, such as implicating other lamp posts like those five mentioned above, as if they had something to do with it.

Truth is, Valentine will benefit, because he is the one they'll go to when they replace the lamps. The bigger problem is how to deal with the cancer. And just what's causing it. You know, you don't take a stethoscope and put it up to a lamp post. You take samples from its skin, its outside, you take a swab of the material, you test it. They'd done that. They knew exactly what's going on there.

She would learn, soon enough, and she was the one who broke the story. She was the one who ran a series of three articles, the first with the headline "Port's Rotten Truth."

When it parsed out, when it played itself to conclusion, fines were imposed, some heads rolled and some changes were put into place. She then went down to see for herself. She went to get her own sense of what they had done to deal with the cancer.

And, of course, she went and saw the five.

There was one who had not said anything before, but this time spoke to her very energetically:

"You are one who can hear us. We want to thank you. The five of us are family. I look at these four as brothers and sisters We look after each other. But for your getting the truth out there, who knows what would have happened. We were next, I am sure of that. We would have gotten it; just a matter of time. So, thank you. I also want you to know, and I want you to try to make sure all of you know, if you have a responsibility for something you made, or that requires your attention to survive, to have any chance of lasting, you've got to tend to it. You all are big on gardens. You know full well if you don't keep at it, weeds are going to find their way in. Weeds are going to have their way. You know full well, you know better than we do, the world you live in, even if far from this port, in fact all over this planet, if you don't take good care of your garden, cancer is going to get it one way or another. There are all sorts of cancers, right? Some are physical. Some are hate. Some are injustice. You think I'm just making a big speech here? You know exactly what I'm saying! Write that, please get that out there, put that in a headline!"

She had not written down a thing. She had no immediate response. She went home and worried about her family. She looked at her kids. She kept thinking about what the lamp post said:

You know full well, you know better than I do, that whole world you live in, even if far from this port, overseas, all over this planet, if you don't take good care of your garden, cancer is going to get it one way or another.

PONDER

Fourteen years. Like clockwork. That's a big expression around here, by the way. (There's a large clock on the top of the main building adjacent to the west side of the square.)

The clock is a bit nosey. And, no pun intended, he often gets very wound up. Among the lamp posts he is considered "to have more than one screw loose." Someone else remarked, "Doesn't keep the best time in the neighborhood..."

Oh... sorry, let me introduce myself.

Lorenzo. My name is said with a real flourish, as in: I am the center of the square. I am the nucleus. The center of the universe. So, if you think of the square as the world, the clock is the sun. Higher windows lit at night can serve as the stars. There are four very fine, stalwart lamps, each at a corner, and then...there's me. Taller, biggest, brightest. Not just as I see it. I am in fact physically larger, physically wider, and shine a bit more brilliantly... In the very center of the square. Think of me as your home planet.

You may ask: What turns me on?

No, I am not making a joke. The question to be asked is not what turns me on, but who?

You do not know the origin of your universe, from what I can tell. You have different ideas about who you worship, if any one, if any thing. I am fully entitled after all this time to try to find out from whence comes my spirit, my life. I am not asking about who made me. I am asking who lights me. I come on without visible effort. It is, as I said above, like clockwork. There has been no occasion yet when I did not light.

We have ways to explore. We can send out feelers, you might say. But, no one has ever answered.

"They set it up somehow. They have computers. Computers are machines that can do things that mimic humans. They can switch on a light, they can clean a floor, they can calculate an amount..."

"Can they communicate?"

"And they can communicate."

So, I am left to ponder. I have ample time when I am awake, a good portion of each day (and night). I notice other lights do not have quite the same routine. In the buildings – those lights come up at varying times – in various windows. My friends who dot the corners of the square, they come on typically in a sequence, a brief time apart.

There are occasions when we are not fully prepared to be turned on. Again, this is not meant to evoke chuckles. This is not funny for us. When I say "turn on" I mean my light glistens like a bright star, perched at the top of my neck. My face is not quite my fortune, my pretty maid, but my bulb certainly is…

There are several theories advanced for what brings me to life. First, that it is willed by a power greater than we can know. An unfathomable force.

Second, that all that exists is the creation of an enormous explosion, setting pieces far and wide, drifting for more years than anyone can imagine, and randomly over time, forming on occasion into life forms, into planets, trees, animals, rivers, mountains, oceans, lamp posts…

I am not convinced by random theory. I don't find a lack of design. Quite the contrary, it seems to me that whatever it is that brings me to life each day involves an elaborate consciousness. It knows me, but apparently I am not able to know *it*. I wish very much I could stop some who walk by, who sit near me. I wish very much I could reach out, find out, and finally know.

There is conjecure that there is a mother source; a basic place from which life springs. What I wonder, what I ponder, is what would it be like not to be brought to life on any given day? Would I know that I have not been brought to life? If so, is that the final moment?

There is a man who a few times a week sets-up within ear shot. He makes great gestures and talks loudly, at times hurriedly, and with great emotion. He shouts, "The world is not yours to clutch, to siphon, to harm! No, the world is a gift…It is on loan…God is the source of all of this! God is our salvation! Turn to the Lord, not away! Embrace and cherish your gift, this planet, do not cast it aside, or take anything for granted, or tear at its limbs! All that is good comes from on high!"

I would like to meet this God…

But, there is so much to ponder, and often so little that is clear.

Did you know when a lamp post goes out it can indeed come back to light? You sleep, you wake. You are born, later you pass.

Did you know that although our light may sometimes flicker, it can be rejuvenated to a light that basks for countless more hours without any interruption?

Did you know that we prefer to be on, not off?

There are some who find greater solace in darkness, who prefer to be off... who whine when they are back on. For me, I want to be around those who vastly prefer light.

I have pondered, perhaps you have as well: If there was no light, would we be able to see?

Well, all right... enough then.

Thank you for listening. I would sure appreciate it if you could help me find who it is, day after day, after day, after day, and then after night, who brings me to light. I have a feeling that it will turn out to be the same force, or phenomenon, or spirit that wakes you each day as well.

So there it is – we do indeed have something in common... that mystery which brings us to life.

APPRECIATION

Unlike trees in any given instance, we are not at all likely to be uprooted by the elements.

We do not complain.

We are not high maintenance, all things considered.

People can utilize us as places to meet, or to indicate distances, and to help them find other locations.

Lamp post marks the spot. You are standing near me, and I near you. We are here.

We also help by providing light.

We are generous to all. We do not discriminate on the basis of anything. We might as well be blind. Light is what we provide, at certain times; perhaps at all necessary times. You get the light come heck or high water. Speaking of which, never has a flood been as tall as my light.

We don't catch fire, at least I have no knowledge of any lamp post ever catching fire. Or cursing.

Signs are placed on us, giving notice, information, offering something, or beseeching.

We are useful – bottom line.

Do you have an appreciation for us?

Do most?

Never gave it much thought?

Is it too fanciful to suggest that we could be pals? Is it so ridiculous to converse with a lamp post?

I see…

Well, then, I have met those of you who are often referred to as, "the unique one in every family…."

Men and women, boys and girls, each with a distinct outlook…talking with me.

Should they have their vitals checked?

Vitals. Interesting expression.

Lamp posts, by the way, don't wink. On occasion we may blink, yes.

We don't fret at all, if you wrap ribbons around us, garlands of some kind, streamers, flags, flowers, tether balls, balloons. We certainly don't fidget!

How much do you even have to feed us? Or clothe us?

We don't steal. Don't rob. Don't burgle.

We provide security to some appreciable degree, no? In some places you would not walk at night if there weren't satisfactory lamp posts, right?

The biggest show-off (by the way) is a lighthouse. Many think, many assume, the lamp post and the lighthouse are related.

We are not.

They are an entirely different species.

Nor are we any other kind of lights, such as those at a ballpark, or spotlights, or street signals.

Holiday lights are seasonal. Not us.

We indeed have a level of uniformity, despite sizes or shapes, or number of bulbs. We are predictable!

There should be an awards show for lamp posts. I am advocating it. Based on merit, and with different categories.

One for those downtown. One for those in residential. One for those at the harbor. One for those in the countryside. One for those along the freeway. One for those in the square. One for those along the board walk. One for lamp posts outside taverns. One for the dancer in the rain. One for those in the theater.

Lamp posts really ought to be part of time capsules.

But, are we too big for a time capsule? Then photos of us should be preserved for all time!

Look: We tell history. We've been around quite a long time. We are not extinct, nor is there much likelihood we ever will be (whether or not you humans figure out a way to stop knocking each other off)…

There should be curricula about us.

We have our own belief system, in case you did not know.

Well, ok, just wanted to say I think there should be much greater appreciation for lamp posts. We don't want to be taken for granted any more than you do.

With that: Always, always, we hope you are blessed with light. And to the extent we can, we will help to make it so!

FAMILY ALBUM

Diversity is the spice of life, is it not?

We come in all sizes and shapes, modes and moods.

We are saying hello, however we can.

Do stop by when you get a chance, we're actually good company, or intend to be.

Here is our assorted family album.

Aunt Karen has tried to convince the tree to diet but he just doesn't listen!

Let there by light! (Ok, fine, and some snow on occasion too). As long as we can help you find your way.

Francis is convinced she's the one who inspired Simon &
Garfunkel, and we know well enough not to disagree.

My dad's sister Catherine. She's the non conformist in the family.

Peak a boo!
(Geoffrey is the mischievous one).

Mom and dad, when they started out, with the kids in tow.
Dad used to say "It's a living... and the view is great!"

We love this family. The Brights. They live pretty far away now but we manage to keep in touch. The amazing thing is how well they all still get along.

Barry, Ricky and Stan. They get along great with Catherine. Latest rumor is the three of them might start up a band with Catherine as lead light.

Teddy, hates when the tether ball hits him, but so it goes. He's very philosophical about it all.

Grandpa, retired Colonel Tony. You gotta salute him — he makes sure you do!

My older brother Austin. He is a very serious person.
Very proud no one, not a soul, has ever fallen on his watch.

Our neighbor Tess. She looks pretty small here, but you get closer she stands out!

The long and winding road. That's me up there. Come say hi when you get a chance.

CPSIA information can be obtained
at www.ICGtesting.com
Printed in the USA
FSOW04n0922280417
33640FS